On a Kinky Monday
- Vol. 9 -

S.B.

Disclaimer

This is a work of fiction. Names, characters, business, events, and incidents are the products of the author's imagination. Any resemblance to actual persons, living or dead, or actual events is purely coincidental. All characters are over 18.

A good Monday is a hypnotic Monday.

Thank you to all patrons of Spell… B-O-U-N-D.

for believing in my creativity.

Table of Contents

Introduction

A week is never complete without a bit of fetish fun, so if you've come here looking for it, you're definitely in the right place.

In the ninth volume of this micro-fiction series, you'll find fifty-six new pieces of micro-fiction where pretty much anything is possible as long as someone loses their mind. These are tales involving femdom, femdom hypnosis, mind control, succubi, goddess worship, lesbian relationships, hypnotic amnesia, human statues, videogames, movies, pet play, feminization, and countless other themes you'll love to explore time and time again.

The pieces in this collection were written during the months of May and June 2022 as part of the Micro-Fiction Monday feature on my Patreon feed. More volumes will be appearing throughout the remainder of the year.

Have fun.

A Chance to Escape

"He's mine, Agnes!"

"I saw him first, Miranda."

"I don't care. He's still coming with me."

"Over my dead body, bitch."

"That shouldn't be too hard, considering you're already dead."

"So are you. Do you think you're better than me?"

"I'm sure I am. Now go back to the shadows and let me have my prize."

"I already said no. If you want him, you'll need to fight for it."

"Oh, you want a piece of me, huh? Is that it?"

"Bring it on, slut."

The two horny demons engaged in a furious exchange of tail swipes and poisoned claws while Thomas watched. Common sense told him it was a good time to make a quiet escape, yet his cock urged him to enjoy the show while it lasted. Guess which voice he listened to.

A Changed Woman

Diana's house looked completely different since the last time her sister Sidney had been there.

"You've redecorated," she said.

"I did. Do you like it?"

"It's… strange. It doesn't seem like your style at all."

"I'm a changed woman. I like new things now."

"Such as…?"

"Hypnosis, BDSM..."

"How did that happen?"

"Do you know when you meet someone that rocks your world? That's how. Mistress takes good care of me now."

"Oh wow! Will I get a chance to meet this Mistress of yours?"

"Absolutely. I invited her for dinner tonight because she can't wait to meet you too."

Sidney stared at her sister. For a moment, she thought she saw an evil smirk creeping on her lips but surely it was just a trick of the light. What could go wrong?

All Together

It had taken a lot of effort, but the choir was finally ready for action and their first performance following the reopening of St. William's Church was sure to impress.

Word spread out, and the flock rushed in, dozens of men and women united in the desire to find meaning in a higher purpose again. It was the first time the church had ordained a female minister, but the surprises were only just beginning.

Dressed in black and gold, Ava greeted everyone with a smile before hitting the keyboard for the first hymn. Her powerful voice joined the choir in an unforgettable introduction. All together, they sang,

"Praised be the Goddess

and her entrancing call.

Praised be the Goddess

Who makes slaves of us all."

One by one, the faithful chosen dropped to their knees and joined in mindless adoration.

A New Board

Victor's King had exhausted all possibilities of defense and was now running for his life in the hope of a fortuitous stalemate and although Beth loved the chase, she wanted things to be over quickly.

"Why aren't you resigning?" she asked, promoting yet another pawn. Three white Queens were overkill, and yet…

"I never do that. You'll have to catch me first," he replied.

"You're simply delaying the inevitable. Are you afraid of what I'll do to you once I win?"

"Considering where the pieces ended up last time, yes."

"Why do you keep betting against me, then?"

"Because you're always entrancing me to do it."

"True…" she chuckled as she moved in for the kill. They were going to need a new board.

A Promise Kept

The Henderson's family gatherings usually ended in hypnotic shenanigans and Rachel was the one to blame. The youngest of three girls and two boys, she was the greatest hypnotist West of the Mississippi (or so she said) and everyone else was slightly afraid of her.

"Not this year, okay?" her brother Anson said. "Promise me you won't hypnotize anyone over dinner."

"I promise," she declared, and for a moment, he actually believed her.

Dinner went by without a hitch, but when dessert came, everyone inside was surprised by the arrival of the entire neighborhood. All men and women had forgotten their clothes at home.

"What the fuck?" Anson gasped. "Rachel, you promised!"

"I know, and I kept my promise."

"Then how do you explain this mess?"

"I entranced them all before coming here," she chuckled. Bob continued to rage, dead to the world.

Are You Awake?

"Honey, are you awake?" Allison asked.

"I am now," Judy grumbled. "What's wrong?"

"I was thinking of hypnotizing you again…"

"In other words, you woke me up to put me to sleep. How ironic!"

"I suppose… Is that so bad?"

"Hmm, honestly, I'd rather be dreaming than having this conversation."

"What if you're already dreaming?"

"Huh?"

"Maybe you're already entranced, and this moment is a part of the fantasy I'm weaving for you."

"You're just saying that to confuse me and put me under more easily, but you know what would really be unexpected?"

"What?"

"If you were the one being hypnotized instead."

"Yes, you're probably ri…"

Judy snapped her fingers, and Allison didn't bother her again for the rest of the night.

Beautiful Day

Thomas smiled, staring at the calendar on the wall.

The best part about Mondays was being hypnotized by his Mistress.

The best part about Tuesdays was being hypnotized by his Mistress.

The best part about Wednesdays was being hypnotized by his Mistress.

The best part about Thursdays was being hypnotized by his Mistress.

The best part about Fridays was being hypnotized by his Mistress.

The best part about Saturdays was being hypnotized by his Mistress.

The best part about Sundays was being hypnotized by his Mistress.

Today was… was… who the fuck cared, anyway? He took off his clothes, wrapped the leather collar around his neck, and waited for her to arrive. It was going to be a beautiful day no matter what.

Be Right Back

"Are we really doing this?" Paul asked.

"Yes," Janice replied. "Trust me, it will be fun."

"Hmm... Human statue still seems extreme to me."

"If your subconscious believes that, the suggestion won't work. Give it a go at least, okay?"

"Okay. What do you need me to do?"

"The same as always. Look into my eyes, relax..."

Paul stared into her gorgeous blue eyes, mind going blank. No matter how many times it happened, going under never stopped being strange. Fingers snapped, and he found himself standing immobile, fully aware of what was happening, yet unable to move a muscle.

Janice was pleased with her success and kissed his frozen lips. And then when the thrill was gone, she said the words he didn't want to hear,

"I need to hit the supermarket. I'll be right back."

The front door slammed shut as he remained helpless in place. Ten minutes passed, then an hour, two…

It's been half a day already. The statue keeps waiting, a warm yellow puddle on the carpeted floor.

Best Money

The bidding for the last item of the auction was going on forever. Bored, Gail declared,

"One hundred million dollars."

Everyone present gasped. What was she thinking?

"One hundred…" the auctioneer choked. "Do I hear one hundred million and one?"

Absolute silence. The young heiress smiled.

"Sold!" he declared, concluding the proceedings.

As everyone was getting ready to leave, Gail reached for the silver jewel and said,

"I'll be taking my possession now."

"I'm sorry, Miss Thorpe, but not until the paperwork is taken care of. How will you pay for the item?"

"I won't. Mr. Harper, you know the legends about this necklace, don't you?"

"Of course, but mind control isn't real. You can't just grab it and leave."

"Are you sure?"

Gail was all smiles when she left the auction house, leaving a trail of masturbating zombies whimpering on the floor. It was the best money she never spent.

Broken

Everything was quiet in Hannah's house. Too quiet. She walked the lonely corridors waiting for something to jump at her at any moment, yet nothing came. Loneliness surrounded her like a death shroud, and she fell to the ground, on the verge of tears.

Everyone was gone. Neighbors, friends, family. They had all left her to cry alone in the darkness and they would not be coming back. What was left except the maddening abyss waiting to claim her?

"Shh, relax, I'm here," she heard Joan's voice inside her mind. "I'm always here for you as long as you give in…"

Hannah stood up, eyes roving the blackness. Joan, of course! How could she have been so stupid? Mistress took care of her property. Mistress would let nothing bad come to her.

"I'm ready," Hannah declared, eyes rolling over as she finally surrendered her identity to her kidnapper's will. Nothing would stop her reprogramming now.

Bullseye

The game was not going according to planned and Richard was getting annoyed.

"Fuck this shit!" he exclaimed.

"What's the matter?" Diana asked. "I thought you were good at darts…"

"I am, but why can't you have a normal target like everyone else?" he pointed at the spiraling red and black mess hanging on the wall.

"Because normal is boring, dear, and you're way more fun when you're hypnotized…" she kissed his right cheek.

"I'm not hypnotized."

"Not yet. Shall we go for another round? Double or nothing this time."

"Sure… bring it! I'll trash you so hard you'll regret this day for the rest of your life."

"Don't count on it," she chuckled as his movements became more and more erratic, brown eyes fluttering. The center of the spiral was waiting for his mind, and the spiral always won.

Business is Booming

As much as Judith loved to look at Claire's statues, there were always a few that freaked her out with how realistic they were.

"You're getting better and better, my friend," she said, staring into the cold eyes of a naked angel. "Any luck with sales lately?"

"Thank you," Claire replied. "And yes, business has been booming since the beginning of the year."

"Oh? What changed?"

"I figured out what people want, I guess."

The two women continued to walk through the studio until they reached the farthest corner where Claire's latest commissions were on display.

"That one looks like your sister," Judith remarked.

"I know."

"And is that your father, too?"

"Yep."

"Weird… it's almost like they're breathing…"

"Really?" Claire produced a syringe from behind her back.

Candie

The sugary treat swirled inside Vicky's mouth as she said, blank-eyed,

"I want candy."

"Of course, you do, sweetie. How coud you not?" asked the gorgeous redhead in front of her. "But I think you wanted to say something else next…"

"I want Candie," Vicky moaned, drowning in the wonderful liquid center.

"Hmm, yes… makes sense, doesn't it? And yet, there's something that's not quite right and you know it. What's your name again?"

"I am Candie…" Vicky declared, overwhelmed by the hypnotic flavors dripping down her throat.

"Yes, that's it! Perfect! You are my Candie. That's all you've ever been. What do you do to please me?"

"Anything you wish, Mistress. Your doll obeys."

"Such a good doll… strip for me. I'm in the mood for a show."

Candie nodded happily, hands on her breasts. One private dance today, a dozen public spectacles tomorrow. She was about to make her new owner a lot of money.

Contaminant

"Alexandra?"

"Yes, General?"

"I know you were supposed to return from vacation today but don't come to the base. There's a contaminant on the loose."

"What sort of contaminant?"

"Unclear but there are a lot of fluids going on here at the moment, so you better stay clear until the situation is cleared."

"Fluids? You need to be more specific, Sir. What's really happening there?"

"I… hmmm… everyone is ejaculating uncontrollably, okay? Damn it! I can't believe I said that out loud."

"Cute. That sounds like something I would do as a hypnotic prank…" she smirked.

"You're right, it does! Alexandra, when did you…? Alexandra, are you still there?"

"Bye for now, General, and thank you for the extra days off."

He hung up the phone, hands on his forehead, a puddle of fresh cum at his feet.

Deeplomatic

The first round of negotiations between the two warring factions went better than expected, but it was the second one that made the headlines. The people around the world won't soon forget the massive orgy that took place while the cameras were rolling.

Only one person didn't engage in the sexual frenzy, and it was none other than UN Representative Dr. Marina Salazar. When asked what happened, the South American blonde faced the reporters with a mischievous smile and said,

"The tension was at an all-time when we began this morning, so I used my hypnotic expertise to de-escalate the situation, but it seems both delegations are incredibly suggestible."

Following the surprising revelation, even more questions came her way, all of them at the same time. "Hypnosis? What did you do? What was the suggestion you used, Dr. Salazar?"

"The obvious one. Make love, not war," she winked.

They did it again the next day, and the next, and the next… The reporters played their part, too.

Demonstration

"Please, Mistress…" Charles begged.

"Please what?" Lucy asked.

"Please! I need it so badly!"

"What do you need, slave? Tell me."

"I need to cum."

"Do you? Hmm, I may allow it if you do it right here…"

"But Mistress…"

"No buts, slave. Are you my hypnotized bitch or not?"

"Yes, Mistress. I'm your hypnotized bitch. I'll do whatever you want."

"Prove it. Stroke and cum at my feet. That's an order!"

"Yes, Mistress," Charles helplessly shot his load before her, humiliated beyond belief.

His parents remained static by the kitchen table, unsure of what the hell they had just witnessed.

"Well…" Lucy smirked. "Now that you know what I do for a living, shall we eat?"

Unsurprisingly, they weren't hungry anymore.

Development Hell

"Okay, guys, I'm really worried here," the company owner said. "I've given you everything you wanted, and the game is still stuck in development hell! Seriously, what's happening?"

"Well," the senior game designer said. "Do you remember 'The Hypnodomme', that enemy type you begged us to include no matter what?"

"Of course."

"It's working too well, and nobody gets any work done because of it," the lead programmer said.

"What do they do then?"

The company owner was given a glimpse of the explosion of cum taking place in the offices below and gasped,

"Oh…"

"Yeah, now if you'll excuse us…"

"Where are you going?"

"To finish the job, obviously."

The game remains unfinished, but their hands have never been softer.

Essay

The deadline was fast approaching, and Jules was at the end of his tether.

"Fuck! I'm never getting this done in time!" he grumbled.

"What's wrong?" his twin sister, Abby, asked.

"Mistress asked me to write an essay about the things I'm willing to do for her, but I'm stumped."

"Why? Don't you want to please her?"

"Of course, I do but the words won't come out."

"Shh, relax… look into my eyes, Jules. Only my eyes… They will help you focus. You know everything is right when you stare into my eyes…"

"I… yes, Abby."

"Very good, always the perfect subject. You will find the words and they will find you. Think of your Mistress, of how much you adore her and then write. Write, Jules. Write for her… and for me."

Jules nodded silently, fingers ready at the keyboard. Mechanically, he typed in capital letters.

"I WILL OBEY MY MISTRESS WITHOUT QUESTION."

"A perfect start," Abby caressed his hair as he fell deeper into a trance.

Every Day…

Every day, Jade entered the winding alleyway two blocks away from her home as she returned from work.

Every day, she felt compelled to go a little deeper inside before snapping out of it and running away.

Every day, she dreamed of what she would find if she stopped being scared of taking one more step into the darkness, and then she would wake up all wet and tingly.

Every day, she said to herself this was the day where her dreams would finally become true.

Every day, the unspoken horror hiding at the end of the alley continued to push its influence deep inside her mind, waiting for her to break. It would have a new thrall soon.

Exciting Enough?

The presentation was utterly boring, not a single game worth buying. Nathan turned off his computer and said,

"That's it, I'm done!"

"What do you mean, done?" Alice asked.

"These things don't speak to me any more. I need something different."

"Like what?"

"I was thinking we could finally try that hypnosis and brainwashing thing you suggested."

"Really?"

"Yeah, can you bring back the excitement again?"

Alice guided him to the kitchen where an apron and a set of cleaning utensils lay in waiting. His heart skipped a beat.

"Is this exciting enough for you?"

"It's wonderful! If I start now, we can do the hypnosis later, right?"

"Sure, dear," she grinned. "Get busy!"

He did. Kitchen today, living room tomorrow, and not a single distraction in his mind. Domestic servitude never felt better.

Fast and Dirty

Erika glanced at the stopwatch and smiled. Ten seconds. Quite the improvement over previous sessions but there was still a lot of work ahead.

"Not bad," she said. "Not bad at all. However…"

"I can go lower," Martin declared.

"You sure can, and you will, right? When my friends come to visit next month, you need to be at the top of their game to impress them."

"It shall be as you say like always. I won't let you down."

"Hmmm, I love it when you talk dirty. Are you ready to continue?"

"Yes, Erika."

"Good," she reached for her favorite pendant. "You already know how this goes. Watch it swing round and round… round and round…"

The month went by quickly, records being broken all the time. From ten to eight, eight to four, embracing the hypnotic humiliation with a smile. When Erika's friends finally showed up,. he was already the fastest premature ejaculator in the world.

Five More Minutes

"It's time, Jeff," Amanda declared.

"Just five more minutes," he asked.

"No. We have a schedule to keep and that's what we'll do. Move along!"

"But I was having such a wonderful dream…"

"You're about to get an even better one."

Bullshit! The chambers in the room upstairs were home to nothing but thoughts of capitulation. Individuality was forbidden in favor of a collective drone nature, and he hated it.

"I don't want to go."

"There's nothing you can do about it, 217," she concluded, using the number that had already sealed his fate. "And you're having company today."

"What company?"

He screamed when he saw the face of his sister suspended in liquid, but it was already too late for her.

Free Again

It had finally happened! The Goddess of the Underworld had found a new vessel and was now commandeering its body like a puppet.

"Tell me what has become of this plane of existence since My imprisonment," She commanded.

"Yes, Goddess," the High Priestess of Hakat replied, ecstatic in her subservience. "Men have taken over everything. Patriarchy is deeply rooted in every corner of the society, and it is believed it will never be eradicated for good. You're needed more than ever."

"Yes, it seems that way," the dark deity muttered, the eyes of her human receptacle flashing red. "We'll see how they feel when they're all brainwashed and kneeling at My feet."

Hakat stepped out into the night, breathing true freedom for the first time in millenia. There was a lot of work ahead to rebuild the world in Her own image.

Fucking Hot

Anna opened her eyes and glanced at the handwritten note on her nightstand. It read, "JUMP". Immediately, she stood up in bed, leaped once and then continued her daily routine as if nothing had happened.

She headed to the bathroom. Stuck on the mirror was another note with a single word. "KNEEL", it said, and she complied without thinking. A few minutes later, she got up, washed her face, and descended to the kitchen.

Her girlfriend Rachel had already left for work, but not before leaving her another command. Atop the counter, lay a camera, a zucchini and one last note that wanted her to "FUCK".

Anna spread her legs and smiled, pussy dripping on the floor. Being a programmed hypnoslave was so fucking hot!

Good Pets

"Is it serious, Dr. Walters?" Tifanny asked.

"Not at all. It's just a minor rash caused by the collar. The pup will be fine."

"Good. Everyone in the house was getting worried sick."

"What about you?"

"I don't do that."

"Why not? He's your responsibility."

"It's just an animal, Dr., and there are plenty others out there."

"Tiffany, anyone that thinks that way, doesn't deserve a pet, but a lesson. Greta, do you mind?" Dr. Walters motioned her assistant.

Something wet assaulted Tifanny's nostrils, and she collapsed on the floor of the veterinary clinic. Three hours later, she woke up in a dark basement, locked in a metal cage that was almost too small for her.

"Let me out of here!" she screamed.

"Not until you change your ways," Dr. Walters declared, turning on a set of multi-colored lights. Good pets need good owners. She would learn her place.

Greatest Writing in the World

It was done. After working all day, Margaret had finally completed her manuscript, and it was bound to change her life forever.

"I want you to be the first person to read it," she said.

"Are you sure?" Nicholas asked.

"Absolutely. Go ahead."

The first sheet of paper read, "You".

The second sheet of paper read, "Must".

The third sheet of paper read, "Sleep".

The fourth sheet of paper read, "For".

The fifth sheet of paper read, "Me".

The sixth sheet of paper read, "Slave".

Nicholas collapsed at her feet, not a care in the world.

Help a Friend

"Come on, Gary!" Oliver pleaded.

"No."

"Please, won't you help a friend out? It's just this once, I promise!"

"You said that last week, and the week before. I won't keep financing your nasty habits!"

"Nasty habits? You make it sound like I'm doing drugs or something!"

"It's almost the same thing. You're addicted to Goddess Angelica's hypnosis, my friend."

"That's preposterous!"

"If so, you won't have a problem going another week without a session, right?"

"No, I can't!"

"What did you say?"

"I can't wait so long! I need my Goddess! I love her, I want to be hers for the rest of my life!"

"That's my good boy..." Goddess Angelica cooed, still pretending to be Oliver's best friend. Programming him undercover was so much fun!

I Know What You Are

Gary struggled against the straight jacket yet remaining completely powerless at what was to come. No mental institution could erase the truth he would never stop shouting,

"I know what you are!" he shrieked. "What you all are!"

"If you do, then you won't be surprised by what happens next…" Dr. Marjorie Adams, a dark-haired vixen with a surprisingly deep voice, replied as she shoved a handful of colorful pills down his throat. "Relax…"

"Demon!" he growled, trying to bite her right index finger off. "You'll never control my mind. I will not be enslaved!"

"Who said anything about that?" she slapped him. "You're too feisty to be servant material, but you'll make a fine appetizer during the next council. Now sleep. I'll check how tender you are again first thing in the morning."

"NO!" he shouted to the padded room until he was all tears and snot. No one cared.

Illusions

There are no words here.

You are not reading this.

Everything you think you're seeing right now is only in your head, and the same goes for everything you're certain was real yesterday.

These sentences are figments of your imagination.

My voice inside your mind is an illusion as well. It can't be anything else.

No one is being brainwashed by their computers at work.

The spirals on the screen were never there.

Your female co-workers did not get together to turn you into a perfect obedient bitch.

Relax. Everything is perfect. You are safe and in peace.

Sleep.

Impfected

It was the strangest D&D campaign Jake and his friends had ever experienced.

"Please, make it stop!" he screamed as his left hand started mutating into a horrible claw while Laetitia laughed.

"I can't. The transformation is irreversible once it's underway. Soon, you'll be reborn again as a mindless thrall to the mighty Dark Queen," she replied.

"This was supposed to be just a game…" he growled, eyes turning red.

"And it is, but it's one in which I always win!" She turned to the other players. "Don't keep me waiting, boys, or things will only get worse from now on."

Trembling, the other three men gathered around her, hoping that the session would be over soon. Unfortunately for them, the young witch had the whole week planned.

No one heard their screams.

Indefinitely

Hello, pets,

how are you all doing? I'm great. In fact, I've never been better. Now, I said I would return from holiday today but I'm having so much fun doing nothing I've decided to prolong my time off indefinitely. I've already booked a cruise around the world and after that, I think I'll just go for another unless I eventually get fed up. It's bound to take a while, though. So… here's what's going to happen. Since you're all so madly in love with me and have no choice but to do as I say, you'll fund these new vacations. The moment you read this message, I expect a hefty tribute to pay for my luxuries, and for those of you that are more suggestible, you are to forget what you did the moment you obey, so you feel compelled to do it again and again… This is how the game is played, even if you don't always remember it. Get busy and see you whenever I'm in the mood for it. Obey!

Last Subject

Lucy stopped by Abner's cubicle and said,

"Just one more week, huh?"

"Yeah. I can't wait," he replied.

"Have you decided where you're going to spend these vacations?"

"A long time ago," he showed her a series of paradisiac images on his computer screen.

"Bermuda? Oh, you'll love it out there. Well, enjoy."

"Thanks, I will."

She left him daydreaming about his upcoming time in the sun and returned to her office where a red phone lay in waiting. She picked up and said,

"Good morning, Dr. Tanner. Yes, I've narrowed down the last subject for your Slave Program. His name is Abner Hawkins, a bit of a loner, and no one will notice his absence. Just make sure to give him memories of a trip to Bermuda once you're done. I'm looking forward to seeing the results this time. Goodbye."

Lucy stretched her arms and legs and yawned. For a moment, she almost felt sorry for Abner. Almost.

Late Again

Natalie was late again, and she didn't know why. With forty-five minutes to spare when she left the office, and practically no traffic on her way to Shanice's place, why was she already fifteen minutes behind schedule?

She parked the car and glanced at her golden wristwatch once more. Of all the presents her girlfriend had given her in their first year together, it was the one she loved the most. Everything about it was luxurious, intoxicating, and hypnotic.

"Hypnotic," she mumbled, half-sleepy eyes reflected on the timepiece's face. Silently, she drifted into trance again.

Almost two hours later, Natalie finally arrived at her girlfriend's place, unsure of how many more times she had gone under.

"Someone's a lot more suggestible than usual today," Shanice welcomed her with a huge grin. "Good. I like that."

So did Natalie, vaginal fluids dripping down her thighs.

Leaked Footage

When Samuel heard the news about "leaked footage" from Adaline's latest music video, he was expecting to see anything but a bald man shooting his load at the camera while she sat on a velvet throne.

"What the fuck is this?" he asked.

His best friend Timothy, who had downloaded the short video from an obscure site earlier that day, finished drinking his soda and replied,

"I told you, it's leaked footage. The new song is called Explosion."

"Nah, not buying it! This looks like porn, and quite the poor one. Adaline is too big of a star to stoop so low."

"It's legit, bro. Look, there's another clip."

Samuel stared at his friend's phone, seeing the exotic artist wrapped in spirals as she sang,

"Come to me as you come for me. Do it now!"

Ten seconds was enough to make him explode once, twice, three times… but rumors claimed the song was at least six minutes long.

"Dear God!" he dropped to his knees, cock and balls hurting with anticipation.

Let Him Be

"Did you see it?" Nathan asked, pointing at the TV.

"No," Bob shrugged. "Are you sure you're okay?"

"I've never been better now that I'm not blind. They're real. You need to believe me!"

"Easy..." Bob said. "Tell me who 'they' are again."

"A female-centric secret society operating all over the world. The group's name remains elusive."

"Right... and they've been brainwashing people into servitude using subliminal TV signals and cell phone antennas, is that it?"

"There are other methods, but those are the main ones, yes. I know I sound like a lunatic, but…"

"But nothing. Go home, Nathan, you're drunk!"

"Bob… please!"

"Get some sleep. It's for your own good."

Bob kicked Nathan out and sighed. His friend was too innocent to get involved in this. If he could convince him he was being delusional, maybe they would be merciful.

Something flashed on the TV screen. Automatically, Bob grabbed his prized baseball bat. So much for letting his friend be. He opened the front door, ready for the hunt.

Magic Isn't Real

Dennis squinted as he watched the impossible lights shooting from Cammie's fingers. What the hell was he looking at?

"What's the trick?" he scoured her bedroom, looking for hidden projectors.

"I already told you there's none. This is all me," she replied.

"So, you're a sorceress now? Come on!"

"Whatever you think of can become true, dear."

"Right… and I'm the Queen of England!"

"If you say so…" she waved her hands and laughed.

"What the…?" he screamed when he saw his wrinkled face in the mirror. "Change it back!"

"Now, do you believe me?"

"I believe everything, okay? Fuck me, that was scary!"

"Fuck you? Sure thing!" she produced a dildo out of thin air.

"Hey, that's not what I… hmmm, deeper please!"

"Gladly."

Dennis hasn't complained once ever since. Who says magic isn't real?

New Lead

It was a sad day for fans of the supernatural procedural show "Deep Dark". After eleven years, main character Rita Tanner was being replaced with a new lead and the complaints online were getting out of the hand.

"Look at this leather bitch they brought in! I hate her already!"

"Deep Dark's producers should all be eating shit for the rest of their lives for killing Rita off."

"Cancellation coming in two weeks, trust me."

The new lead's acting chops left much to be desired, but she had one thing in her favor. Her natural hazel eyes were incredibly bewitching and when she talked, everyone listened. If she said "Sit!", people would sit and if she said "Kneel!" people would kneel. Slowly, the public's perception began to change.

"What a gorgeous woman."

"I love her so much! This is what the show has been needing all this time."

"Marry me, Goddess! Please!"

Ratings have never been higher.

New Vessel

After weeks of hearing mysterious chants coming from her neighbor's basement, Judith finally lost it and decided to take a peek. Sneaking in the dead of night, she saw the congregation in red robes praising a humanoid statue with bright dragon wings and shuddered when its head turned to look straight at her.

She didn't notice her assailants until they were already grabbing her arms and legs and dragging her into the center of the forbidden ritual. The statue called her by name, red eyes glowing within her soul. All vessels were good, but the reluctant ones would always be the most entertaining to control.

Judith's body rose from the floor, arms and legs tainted with blood, looking down at the ecstatic acolytes. Now the fun began.

Outbreak

Dr. Walters was white as a sheet staring at the latest lab reports.

"These numbers can't be right," he mumbled.

"They are, sir," his assistant, declared. "The water supply is tainted."

"How long has this been going on?"

"Based on contamination levels, six months. Everyone has been exposed by now, including us."

"So, the madwoman did it after all…"

"Sir? What are you not telling me?"

"It's nothing, Joe. Can you do me a favor?"

"Sure, Dr. Walters. What is it?"

"Go home early and spend some time with your family, okay? We'll talk tomorrow."

"Now you're scaring me, Dr."

"Tomorrow, Joe. See you then."

His assistant left the office while he drowned in a sea of smoke, reminiscing of his old partner. Gladys was a visionary but also a menace, and even in death, she was still trying to prove her point.

Dr. Walters threw the reports into the garbage bin and reached for his revolver. He had to be ready for the first psychotic outbreak.

Party of a Lifetime

Harold washed his face with cold water for the umpteenth time, trying to stay awake no matter what. It had been almost forty-eight hours since last going to bed, but he needed to keep going otherwise Valerie's suggestions would kick in.

He didn't know what they were this time, but the one thing he had learned about his cousin ever since the first trance was that she enjoyed humiliating him when he least expected. She would do it again when he fell asleep, he was sure of it.

Leaning against the bathroom sink, he yawned yet persevered. He would not fall asleep. He would not…

Harold opened his eyes and suddenly found himself standing inside Valerie's house, wearing a French maid's dress. The party of a lifetime was about to begin, and he couldn't let her down.

Pay the Price

Paul was anything but discrete when something caught, and Marge loved to tease.

"Do you see anything you like?" the redhead saleswoman leaned on the glass counter, giving him a generous view of cleavage.

"Most definitely," he grinned. "The question is how much will they cost me?"

"Oh, honey, these babies aren't for sale."

"Imagine they were."

"You wouldn't be able to pay for them."

"Don't be so sure. I have deep pockets."

"Do you? How deep?"

He opened up his wallet, revealing a collection of credit cards. The black ones were her favorites.

"Is this deep enough?"

"It will be once you give me what I want."

"Which is…?"

"Your mind."

Marge flashed her boobs, and his eyes went blank. He will be paying the price of his cheekiness for the rest of his life.

Plan H Redux

The Voltraxian Commander Fehl-Ghar kneeled before the Emperor of his homeworld, ashamed of his failure.

"Earth still stands, Your Imperial Majesty. I know I don't deserve it, but I beg for Your forgiveness nonetheless," he declared.

"You messed up again? How is this possible?" the feisty monarch asked.

"Do you remember the enemy's secret weapon?"

"That hypno… what's her name? Vaguely, yes."

"The word you're looking for is 'Hypnodomme', Your Imperial Majesty. She was waiting for us once more and this time had friends with her."

"How many of these 'friends' are we talking about?"

"About one hundred or so. They worked together to turn our soldiers into their puppets and steal our ships."

"How did you escape, then?"

"I didn't," the Voltraxian Commander drew his weapon and vaporized the Emperor with a single blast. Mistress Phoebe would be proud.

Power of Suggestion

The test results were out, and all one hundred subjects were performing better than anticipated.

"Please explain to me again what it is I'm looking at," Carmen said.

"It's simple, really," Angie replied. "We told them all their wine had been laced with a hypnotic drug."

"And now they're hypnotized? Why is that special?"

"None of the glasses were tampered with. This is the power of suggestion at its best. Now they believe they have no choice but to obey, so they do it."

"There's nothing extraordinary about that," Carmen scoffed. "Just because you found one hundred gullible individuals for this stupid test that doesn't mean everyone else will fall for the same trick. I'm pulling my funding right now."

"I'm afraid you can't do that."

"Why not?"

"Your wine was laced with a hypnotic drug. On your knees, bitch!"

"Yeah, rig…"

Carmen never finished the sentence. She still hasn't got up either.

Reality is Overkill

The virtual bell rang twice, calling Saul to attention. He dashed away from the bathroom, pants down, and kneeled before his computer screen.

"You must come immediately when you're called," the spiraling letters flashed before his eyes.

"Yes, Mistress," he replied, mind flooded with a wave of hypnotic ecstasy. Ever since Alicia had begun experimenting with the new computer program, his training had become more intense yet easier to follow. Slavish thoughts were always on the back of his mind, ready to be awakened at will but he was certain of one thing: he would never submit entirely no matter what happened. Fantasies were fun but reality was overkill.

"We'll see about that in a couple of months," she said.

Two weeks later, the changes were already permanent. Saul continued repeating the lies of his freedom to himself and sank deeper.

Reign of Terror

The witch cracked a smile as she looked at the paladin from atop her golden throne.

"Back for more so soon? I knew you couldn't stay away from my control for long," she said.

"Your reign of terror ends tonight."

"Does it? And how are you going to stop me from taking over your mind again?"

"The people are with me," he pointed at a roaring crowd coming up the mountain toward her castle.

"And my army of thralls is with me," she declared, clapping her hands. Immediately, hundreds of ravenous servants surrounded him, bloodshot eyes demanding his sacrifice. "You really didn't think this through, did you?"

"Even if I die today, I swear…"

"… you'll serve me forever as yet another mindless zombie? Yes, you will."

The paladin screamed as her pets piled up on him until he forgot how to breathe. Then, they swarmed out of the castle gates to greet the angry townsfolk. The feast lasted all night.

Rejuvenated

Greg's jaw slacked when he realized who was waiting for him in the pool.

"Katherine? You look…"

"Fifty years younger?" she purred.

"Yes. How is this possible?"

"You know how."

"You found her!" he exclaimed.

"Yes, I did, and she made all my wishes come true."

"But at what cost?"

"My soul, eternal servitude… nothing important."

"Nothing imp…? Have you lost your fucking mind?"

"No, only my free will. It's what she wanted and now we're both happy. Join me, Greg. Let's serve her together."

"I can't do that."

"Hmm, right… she told me you would resist, which is why…"

"What? Spill it, Katherine!"

"I didn't come alone."

Through the corner of his left eye, he saw a shadow moving, right before the Vampire' Queen's fangs ripped his throat in half.

Rookie Mistake

The hellish emissary looked at the circle drawn on the floor and then confronted the young woman who had been foolish enough to summon her.

"Let me guess, it's the first time you're doing this, right?"

"No," Valerie shivered on the inside. She couldn't show fear to the fiery creature.

"Hmm, you're trying to pull my leg, but I commend the audacity. Shall I tell you how I know you're a real beginner in this world?"

"No. I don't want to hear your lies."

"It's a good thing I don't lie, then. I see you have all the books, and the circle is almost perfect, but…"

"What do you mean, almost? You're trapped and must do whatever I want, bitch!"

"Actually, no. You added your name to the circle instead of mine. Thank you for giving me explicit permission to possess you, dear."

Dark flames entered Valerie's mouth, nose, and ears.

Selective Amnesia

Eric trembled when he saw Olivia approaching him, holding her favorite pocket watch in her left hand.

"Honey, what you're doing? Didn't we agree that yesterday was the last time?" he asked.

"Did we? I don't remember that at all."

"How can you not? If is this a joke, it's not funny."

"It's no joke, Eric. I don't remember saying that, so it never happened. You're going down for me again."

"No, I don't want to… Wait, I understand what's going on now."

"Do you? Please explain."

"You hypnotized yourself into forgetting what you said so you wouldn't feel guilty about entrancing me again, didn't you?"

"As if I would ever do such a thing…" she smirked.

He never knew for sure. Then again, he didn't remember the rest of the day either.

The Best Movie I've Ever Seen

It was the surprise hit of the season. Critics couldn't get enough of Alana Thompson's first motion picture but there was something unnerving about her success. Every review began with the same sentence, "This is the best movie I've ever seen."

Jim had had enough of such strange idolatry. Both his blog and following were small, but he was always honest. He would see with his own eyes what it was all about and then pass his judgment.

Alone in the comfort of his apartment, he streamed the most chaotic spectacle he had ever seen, one random sequence after the other. None of it made any sense and yet he remained transfixed, blinking with the flashing screen until the credits rolled. When the presentation was over, he couldn't remember a single line or scene from it, but he was absolutely certain of this,"

"This is the best movie I've ever seen," he typed, kneeling before his computer.

The Great Expansion

On the last day of the year 2099, Tabitha Winters disappeared from her home in a ball of blinding light at exactly 3:33 am.

One hundred years later, she appeared in the same place at the same hour to the surprise of the new family living there. She looked almost the same, except for a new pair of golden eyes and anyone that saw her became aroused beyond control.

One by one, all police officers, firemen, and military personnel who tried to stop her, fell to the ground, consecutive multiple orgasms rendering them harmless and powerless. The ecstatic infection spread quickly and, in less than twenty-four hours, two-thirds of the adult population of the world was reduced to a quivering mass.

And so, the Galactic Empire of Inrapta IV peacefully conquered another planet, the powerful Overladies celebrating their cunning in the skies above. The Great Expansion continues.

The Spiral Marks the Spot

Lindsay hated treasure hunts. Going around the city looking for cryptic clues to her next objective was not her idea of fun and she didn't hesitate to say so.

"When will this be over?" she asked over the phone.

"You're almost there," her girlfriend, Andrea, replied. "Are you tired yet?"

"Tired and grumpy. This was the first and the last time, you hear? Never again!"

"I hope you change your mind. I'll be waiting for you at the last stop. See you soon."

Lindsay hung up and looked at the final clue one more time. It wasn't as hard as the others and a simple substitution cypher told her where she needed to go. It was the park where they had first met. When she arrived there, a giant rainbow-like spiral waited for her. She froze in place, her thoughts draining under the weight of unexpected trance.

"Here's your prize," Andrea said. "Was it worth the trouble or not?"

"You can say that…" Lindsay drooled.

"Good." Their lips met in perfect bliss.

Three Hundred Million

GwennDoll was a case of unparalleled success in the online world. Nobody expected her to reach one hundred thousand subscribers in two months or double that count less than thirty days later. With little effort, her brand continued to grow, and no one understood why.

Frank was one such guy. Aged twenty-six, he had long outgrown easy personality cults and would simp for no woman. So what if she looked amazing with purple hair and had the most gorgeous eyes ever? He would never… hmm… never…

"Thank you for subscribing to my channel, Frank," the personalized message on his inbox read. "You did the right thing. You always do the right thing when you watch my videos, listen to my voice, or simply lose yourself looking at me. You will do it right now. Start with my Q & A video, learn the things I love the most and drop deeper and deeper. You will be a good thrall like everyone else."

Frank nodded, beginning his indoctrination right away. Goddess GwennDoll's numbers were still too low. Three hundred million next week was possible. It had to be.

Too Much Power

"I don't get it, I really don't," Daniel grumbled. "You're ugly as sin, you have no sense of style, and listening to your voice is worse than hearing someone scratch their nails on a chalkboard so how the fuck are you so successful and command a legion of mindless simps willing to do anything to to keep you happy?"

Penelope stared at her freshly painted nails, rolled her eyes, and replied,

"I'm a femdom hypnotist," she snapped her fingers and pointed at the ballerina outfit on the floor. "It's your turn to entertain me tonight."

Daniel undid his T-shirt, still fuming on the inside, and immediately got to work. Some people had too much power, while others had none. Resistance was useless. He would obey.

Where Are the Cats?

The noises coming from Alicia's house were driving Danielle insane.

"Okay, where are the cats?" she barged inside the moment her neighbor opened the door.

"I don't know what you're talking about," she replied.

"Don't lie to me. You have cats in the house and the sounds are coming from..." Danielle pressed her hands against a wall, suddenly revealing a secret door to a until then unknown basement. "... here. Hmmm, what is this now?"

"Danielle, wait!"

Too late. The nosy woman descended into the darkness and was confronted by a collection of pretty brainwashed catgirls purring and meowing against metal bars.

"What the hell?" she muttered.

"You weren't supposed to see this..." Alicia stabbed her neck with a syringe. It's a good thing she had an empty cage.

Who?

"How was your birthday, John?" Randy asked.

"Huh?"

"Your birthday, dude! You were so excited about it this year that you even ditched your mates, so… What happened? What did you do?"

"I have no idea what you're talking about."

"Come on, John! What game are you playing this time?"

"It's no game. What birthday? Nothing happened."

"Oh, shit! I think I know what's going on. You spent time with Veronica again, didn't you?"

"Who?"

"Veronica! The cute redhead hypnotist we met at the theater last Summer… You don't remember her either?"

"I don't even remember who you are…" John shrugged.

Randy sighed. Damn, she was good!

You're No Freak

Paul sat in his bedroom, crying. Why couldn't he be normal?

"What did you just say?" Natasha asked, caressing his left hand.

"Why am I a freak?"

"You're not. Why do you think that? Is it because of your submissive nature?"

"Yes. I hate it! I hate it so fucking much!"

"No, you don't," she cooed. "You're simply confused. That's understandable but you'll grow to accept it and once you do, you'll be happier than ever."

"So you say, but I don't believe you. I should have never let you get inside my head."

"I didn't do anything your subconscious didn't desire. In time, you'll be a good servant. Trust me."

Paul fell on his back, bitter tears rolling down his eyes. He didn't want to submit and yet he had no choice. The trance leftovers continued to swirl in his mind, changing his thoughts one by one.

Conclusion

The fantasies of the mind are over for now, but you can expect more volumes in the next months. Until then, be sure to visit keep up with the updates on my personal website - https://www.sbspellbound.net -, for the surprises just keep on coming. Support my creative efforts if you wish to see more and more. Have fun.

www.ingramcontent.com/pod-product-compliance
Lightning Source LLC
Chambersburg PA
CBHW052127150726
48002CB00006B/2518